Contents

Other essential

See page 121 for more details.

Introduction

Have you ever done something so embarrassing that you wish you could turn back time? An episode in your past that still makes your cheeks heat up in shame? Me? I can name a few. All of them involved being drunk, and then saying or doing something supremely daft. Usually in the presence of girls. Somewhere out there, for example, is a photo of the author at a party wearing nothing but his socks and a traffic cone. It's cringe-making stuff, in the sober light of day, but my most embarrassing moment goes beyond being funny, and came to mark the moment in my life when I took a long, hard look at my relationship with drink.

It happened on the way back from a party, at which I'd shared a bottle of horrendously strong cider with my mate, Al. His dad must have known we were plastered when he arrived to pick us up. He didn't say anything about it, but his silence spoke volumes, and I knew for sure that Al was in trouble. So there I was, spinning out in the back seat, wondering what kind of lecture he would get, when my stomach did a frightening flip flop. I knew I wasn't going to make it home, but I was so horrified at the idea of asking his dad to pull over that instead I did the worst thing possible. I leaned forward, opened up the elasticated pocket in the back of the driving seat, and proceeded to be quietly sick.

Now throwing up in the car was one thing. Not saying anything about it was another. I was so mortified that I actually slipped out without a single word of apology, and watched them drive away feeling like the lowest worm on earth.

Next day, I woke up with more than a hangover. It was then I started to question what drink did to me. Not least to my social graces and my self-esteem. Why did I have to get so smashed? Why couldn't I just be myself for a change? And that's exactly what I did. Next time I went out, I made that change. I didn't stop drinking, but I started having some respect for it, and learned to have a good time without falling down. As for my mate Al, we're still good friends although I've never quite been able to look his dad in the eye. That's why this book is dedicated to him, with apologies for the upholstery!

In the UK, 96% of 16 year olds have tried alcohol, while three quarters of all young people admit doing something they regret while drunk. What's more, the amount consumed by this age group has doubled in the last decade. In view of these sobering statistics, here's a book that recognises the role alcohol plays in our lives, and aims to provide a steadying influence. Whatever your outlook on booze, there's no preaching here. Just smart advice, and fast facts to help you make informed decisions without having to make the mistakes.

● CHAPTER ONE ●

Understanding alcohol

"My mates respect the fact that I choose not to drink. It isn't compulsory, after all."

Dominic (15)

"I drink beer to get drunk. It's as simple as that."

Karla (16)

"The first time I tried a glass of red wine, I couldn't understand the attraction. It tasted absolutely disgusting, but the second time was better so I guess there must be more to it than I first thought."

Catherine (14)

Alcohol has been around for thousands of years. There are frequent references in the Bible, while booze played such a big part in Roman times it's a miracle they got it together to conquer anything but their hangovers. Through the ages, alcohol has been banned and bootlegged, quaffed in celebration and commiseration, and even used to sterilise surgical instruments. It's illegal to drink in some countries like Saudi Arabia, while nations like France and Australia are famous for producing fine wine and beer.

"The first time I asked my dad if I could try his gin and tonic, he got all flustered and said no. Then, about a week later, he asked if I'd like to help fix a drink for him. It tasted revolting when he offered me a sip, but we had a laugh about it. Ever since then, *he's* been the one who keeps asking *me* about alcohol. It doesn't really appeal at the moment, but if it does I know I can ask him any questions."

Caitlin (13)

People who drink sensibly enjoy its relaxing effect, and it can help them feel more upbeat and sociable. In moderate amounts, alcohol is associated with fun and laughter, while many find it helps them set aside their day-to-day worries for a short time. Recent studies have even suggested that drinking moderate amounts of red wine can protect against heart disease. Sadly, however, alcohol can become a problem for some when they turn to drink as a way of blotting out difficult or troubling issues in their lives.

WHAT IS ALCOHOL?

OK, here comes the science bit: an alcoholic drink is basically flavoured water with a substance called *ethyl* in it – also known as alcohol. This is made by fermentation with fruits, vegetables or grains. In the process, the natural sugars are broken down and turned to alcohol. People sometimes refer to alcoholic drinks as booze, liquor, a beverage or bevvy.

"My older brother once got really drunk at a wedding. When he surfaced the next day he looked very queasy, but my mum didn't have any sympathy for him. She said he'd brought it on himself."

Paula (13)

Alcohol is found in drinks such as beer, lager, alcopops, wine, cider, and spirits like whisky, vodka or gin. Alcoholic drinks range in strength and are measured as a percentage of the total volume. The higher the percentage marked on the label, the stronger the effect, and people use this information to stay aware of how much they're drinking. For example, a typical lager might contain 5% alcohol, wine 12%, while a spirit such as vodka could score 40%.

WHAT HAPPENS WHEN WE DRINK ALCOHOL?

When you have a drink, the alcohol is quickly absorbed through the stomach lining and into the bloodstream. Within five minutes, it's heading for the brain. Which is where the effects begin to kick in.

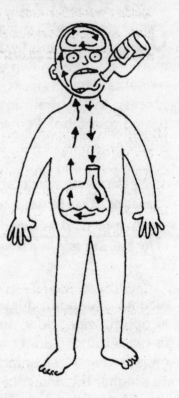

"I've said some stupid things when I'm drunk. It's like your mouth disconnects from your brain, and says whatever you're thinking."

Reece (15)

Alcohol is in fact a depressant drug, which means it slows down brain activity. The frontal lobes are the first bit of your bonce to be affected, although weirdly enough in small amounts alcohol increases a sense of cheerfulness and well-being. Why? Because this is where your self-awareness and impulses are controlled. Continue drinking, however, and your powers of reasoning begin to slide, as does your control of language and memory. Which is why drunken mates always mumble stuff about loving you on the way home, but then deny all knowledge in the morning!

"One time I woke up after a big night out, and I couldn't remember exactly where I'd been. It really made me think about how much I was drinking, and why I always had to go overboard."

Jim (16)

The effects of alcohol on the brain increase with every drink. Next to be hit are the areas that control memory, hunger and emotion. People who are very drunk can go through sudden mood swings, and sadly among men this often results in acts of aggression and violence.

"If you're not careful with drink the effects can creep up on you. People don't call it 'falling down water' for nothing!"

Michele (15)

Extreme levels of drinking can even affect basic body functions, such as breathing and heart rate. The risk of unconsciousness also begins to increase, while vomiting in this state can result in death by choking.

BOOZE BULLETIN

Methyphobia is the medical term used to describe a fear of alcohol.

How much is too much?

The amount of alcohol a person consumes is measured in units. Here are some rough examples of what makes up a typical unit:

- Half a pint of beer, lager or cider
- Half a bottle of alcopops
- A small glass of wine
- A single measure of spirits (e.g. whisky, vodka, rum or gin)

As a rule, health experts recommend that adult men drink no more than 21 units per week, and women 14 units. In real terms, this means men shouldn't exceed two pints of lager/beer, or three glasses of wine a day, while women shouldn't go beyond a pint or a couple of glasses. This is because the male body is made up of 66% fluid, compared to 55% for women. This means alcohol is more diluted in a man's body than a woman's. As a result, women get drunk faster than men on the same amount of alcohol.

BOOZE BULLETIN

Each year, more than 1000 people under 15 are hospitalised with acute alcohol poisoning.

Just be aware that these are guidelines and not targets to aim for. Nor are they intended for young people. It's almost impossible for experts to provide sensible drinking guidelines for under-18s, because people mature physically at different rates. So if you're going to drink, be realistic about how much you can handle.

OTHER FACTORS

It's not just age and gender that have an influence on the effects of drinking alcohol. There are many other factors to consider:

• The type of drink

The body absorbs some alcoholic drinks faster than others. The effects from fizzy drinks such as champagne, alcopops, sparkling wines and cider may be felt much quicker than beer or spirits, and may catch some people by surprise.

"One pint makes me giggly, but things aren't so funny after a few more."

Greg (14)

• The rate you drink

The rate at which a drink is consumed will also determine how quickly alcohol enters the bloodstream. Pacing yourself gives greater control over the effects, and helps you judge when you've had enough.

"My cousin once drank half a bottle of sweet sherry really quickly. He was fine for about ten minutes. Then he went green, and about five minutes later was locked in the toilet throwing up."

Ella (13)

• Your physical build

Your weight, height and size play a big role in determining the effects of alcohol. The bigger you are, the more blood you have in your body, which means the concentration of any alcohol consumed will rise at a slower rate than in a smaller person.

"My friends joke that I can't hold my drink, but they know it's because I'm only little!"

Johnny (15)

• Your tolerance to alcohol

Drinking alcohol changes your body and brain chemistry. You don't need to drink much the first time to feel the effects, but your system can get used to the repeated presence of a drug like alcohol. The more 'tolerant' you become of alcohol, the more you need to drink to get the same effects. This can be dangerous, as you may end up accidentally drinking more than your body can handle, resulting in overdose.

"My uncle never seems to get drunk, but his breath always reeks of whisky."

Ben (13)

• When you last ate

Alcohol is absorbed into the bloodstream through the stomach lining, which is why it's always advisable to eat before drinking.

"Drinking on an empty stomach is the fastest way to ruin a good night out. The alcohol goes straight to your head, and the world soon starts spinning after that!"

Twig (16)

• How you're feeling

If someone is down when they drink, the alcohol will tend to leave them feeling worse. This is due to the fact that alcohol is a depressant drug. It acts on the central nervous system and slows down brain activity. However, it can also mean that people who are otherwise happy and in good spirits will be less prone to becoming aggressive when drunk.

"I've heard that when my girlfriend's ex is drunk he makes threats about how he's going to kick my head in. It's weird, because I've seen him when he's sober and he's been fine with me."

Pete (14)

• Your environment

The effects of drinking alcohol are often more apparent if you're in public at the time and interacting with others. You're also likely to drink more in social situations, especially when others are boozing.

"When you're at a party, just chatting and drinking, it's easy to finish a can of lager without even realising."

Milly (15)

BOOZE BULLETIN

In some parts of Alaska, it's illegal to give a moose an alcoholic drink!

SOBERING UP

The liver is a bit of a snail when it comes to burning up booze. On average, it takes an hour to deal with one unit of alcohol, and as the buzz of being drunk wears off, so the after-effects can kick in. The more you drink, the longer it takes to feel sober again, and the more acute or unpleasant the experience can be. In other words: a hangover. Your body has fought hard to deal with the toxic effects of alcohol, which is why you feel a little worse for wear. Symptoms can include:

- Headache, dry mouth and thirst (signs of dehydration).
- Sickness, nausea and shakiness (signs of falling blood alcohol levels).
- Stomach ache (alcohol is an irritant, and this is a sign that your guts are inflamed).

"The worst part about waking up with a hangover is the fact that people rarely show any sympathy! If you were ill because you'd eaten something dodgy, everyone would go out of their way to let you lie down or take time out!"

Jody (16)

Anyone who drinks will have their own way of dealing with a hangover, but there is no quick-fix solution. Contrary to popular opinion, drinking coffee won't sober you up. It contains a stimulant drug called caffeine, which just makes you feel more awake. Having another alcoholic drink won't help either. This is sometimes called 'hair of the dog', but all it does is stoke up your alcohol levels and make the inevitable hangover that little bit harder to handle. All you can do is tough it out, and drink plenty of water to counteract the dehydrating effect of alcohol (i.e. headaches and fatigue).

"My brother swears that drinking down a raw egg, spiced with hot pepper sauce, is the best way to cure his hangover! Watching him try to keep it down, however, I'm surprised it doesn't just make him sick!"

Eric (13)

BOOZE BULLETIN

Drinks such as red wine or brandy can leave you with a serious headache. This is caused by 'congeners' — a group of substances that are formed during the fermentation process in dark coloured drinks.

ALCOHOL, THE LAW AND YOU

A busing alcohol can be very dangerous, and even fatal. As a result, there are laws governing its sale and consumption in the UK. Here are some of the key points that apply to young people:

- It is illegal for anyone under the age of 18 to buy alcohol.
- If you're under 18, the police may inform your parents if you're caught attempting to purchase alcohol from a licensed premises such as a pub, bar or shop.

- A landlord or shopkeeper who knowingly sells alcohol to someone under the age of 18 faces criminal prosecution.
- You're allowed in a pub or a bar once you're 14, although you can only be served a soft drink. Some places have a licence allowing children under 14 into the bar, but they must have an adult with them.
- A parent or adult responsible for you could be committing an offence if they buy you a drink in a bar or pub. But if you're aged 16-17, and you're eating a meal in a licensed restaurant, then you can legally be served beer or cider.
- It is not illegal to drink at home if you're under 18.
- Under the Public Order Act 1986, it is an offence to possess or carry alcohol on coaches and trains travelling to and from certain sporting events like football matches.
- The police have the power to confiscate alcohol from teenagers found drinking alcohol in a public place, like the street or the park. What's more, if caught doing this you will be obliged to give your name and address or risk a £500 fine.
- It is an offence to be drunk and disorderly in a public place, and that includes licensed premises such as a pub.

BOOZE BULLETIN

Before they were famous, Bruce Willis and Sandra Bullock both earned a living by working behind a bar.

● PUB QUIZ ●

1 **Drinking alcohol can make you:**
   a) depressed
   b) more attractive
   c) happy

2 **How many people regularly drink alcohol in the UK?**
   a) 100%
   b) 64%
   c) 90%

3 **The amount of alcohol contained in a drink is measured by:**
   a) the percentage
   b) the price
   c) the taste

4 **Boozing when you're hung over is the surest way to:**
   a) Forget about your headache
   b) Get drunk again
   c) Make your hangover much worse when it finally kicks in

5 **If you're under 18 and caught buying alcohol, who gets into trouble?**
   a) you
   b) the shopkeeper
   c) you and the shopkeeper

ANSWERS

1: a (depressed)

Alcohol may lift your spirits at first, but it is a depressant drug. Ultimately, if you're feeling down, it will make you feel worse.

2: c (90%)

Drinking is one of the most popular social pastimes in the UK. It's also one of the biggest causes of health problems, which is why it's so important to think about drink and recognise the risks involved.

3: a (the percentage)

Alcoholic drinks come in different strengths, measured as a percentage (%) by volume. The higher the percentage marked on the label the stronger the drink will be.

4: a, b and c (all three!)

A hair of the dog drink won't cure your hangover. It'll increase your blood alcohol level, which might serve to distract you from the fact that you feel so bad, but eventually your hangover will return – and chances are it'll be even worse than before!

5: c (you and the shopkeeper)

A shopkeeper caught selling alcohol to an under-18 may lose his/her licence, while the police may inform your parent/s or carer.

CHAPTER TWO

Why do people drink?

"Everyone drinks, don't they? I'd feel really weird about turning up at a party without a couple of cans of beer."

Saul (15)

"It washes away your nerves, especially when it comes to chatting people up. The downside is you risk talking rubbish, of course!"

Fran (14)

"My dad fixes himself a drink as soon as he gets in. He doesn't even ask how my day was. Not until he has a gin and tonic in his hand."

William (13)

People drink for all sorts of reasons, but mostly because they enjoy it. In moderate amounts the immediate effects of alcohol can help people relax and lower inhibitions, which is why it plays such a big part in our social lives. From bars and pubs to parties, drink brings people together – for better, but sometimes for worse. Either way, here's a breakdown of the draw behind the drink.

TO SATISFY A CURIOSITY

Even if you don't drink, it's impossible to avoid alcohol. Every year, the drinks industry spends roughly £200 million on advertising and sponsorship. From billboards to sporting events and television ads, images of drinking and drinkers surround us. Pubs play a central role in many popular soap operas, while celebrities are often snapped quaffing. It's no wonder we become aware of alcohol from a very early age. So when the opportunity arises to try it for ourselves, the temptation is hard to avoid – and often with whatever alcohol happens to be available.

"I used to help myself to my dad's whisky. It nearly always left me feeling giddy and ill, but I was fascinated by the buzz. My dad sussed me eventually because I kept topping up the bottle with water. He said it wasn't so much that I'd been drinking that upset him as the fact that I hadn't felt able to talk to him about it."

Sean (15)

Some parents encourage their sons or daughters to experience their first taste of alcohol at home. They feel it gives them more control over the situation, and takes away the taboo so everyone feels free to talk about any issues or uncertainties. For many others, however, it's peer pressure that persuades them to experiment with alcohol.

"A couple of my mates got hold of some cider, and were sharing it round to get drunk. It tasted grim to me, but I was too embarrassed to say no."

Jamie (14)

Experts believe your friends can be the biggest influence when it comes to drink and drugs. If your mates are drinking it can be very hard to decline the invitation to join in. That's why it's so important to be aware of the facts about alcohol, and the effects that drinking can have. The more you know, the more confidence you'll have to make informed decisions. It beats just going for it simply because someone you look up to says you should.

TO UNWIND

Like most drugs, alcohol can affect your mood. The vast majority of people who drink do so because it helps them relax. They enjoy drinking, and the feelings associated with it, which is fine providing they stay aware of their relationship with alcohol.

"My dad sometimes goes for a quick pint after work. Mum doesn't mind because she reckons it stops him coming home moaning about his day."

Simone (13)

The bottom line is people have to be honest with themselves about their reasons for drinking. In moderate amounts alcohol may well help you loosen up, but there's always a risk of losing control to it.

TO BE SOCIABLE

Alcohol lowers inhibitions, which means it makes you feel less self-conscious about things you say and do. That's what makes it such a popular feature at any social gathering, from parties to clubs and special occasions like weddings, birthdays and Christmas time.

"With a drink in my hand, I never run out of things to say."

Rob (15)

"My girlfriend asked me why I always got so drunk at parties. I didn't give her an answer, but it really made me think about it."

Nick (15)

BOOZE BULLETINS

- *60% of 13-17 year olds in the UK claim to have bought alcohol in a pub or an off-licence, despite the fact that it's illegal to do so until you're 18.*

- *By the age of 12, the number of people who have tried alcohol begin to outnumber those who haven't.*

If you do drink when you're out with friends, just be aware that it doesn't make you a more interesting, appealing or amusing person. If you can relax and be yourself without alcohol, the end result is the same. Unless, of course, you booze beyond your limit...

"My boyfriend changes when he drinks too much. I see a side to him I don't really like. He can get a bit cocky, and more than once he's tried to show me up in front of his mates."

Jenny (14)

BOOZE BULLETIN

A recent survey found that more than a quarter of young people who drink beer, lager or cider always went for stronger brands.

TO GET DRUNK

Let's be honest, people sometimes deliberately set out to get smashed. More often than not, it's the lads who use alcohol for this reason. Why? Because hard drinking has a certain appeal that's as macho as it is misguided. Sure, it might be a laugh to lose control with mates, but it doesn't exactly impress. Nor does it feel good the next morning.

"I was so drunk on my birthday I don't even know if I had a good time."

Scott (15)

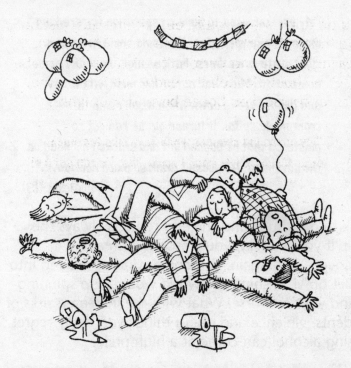

It's fair to say that most young people learn a lot about drinking from their mistakes. Going overboard with alcohol might leave you with a better understanding of your limits, but you have to learn to respect it too.

BOOZE BULLETIN

The term 'honeymoon' comes from an ancient Babylonian wedding tradition, in which the bride's father would supply his son-in-law with all the mead he could drink for the first month of their marriage. Mead is a beer made with honey, and the term 'honey month' soon became 'honeymoon'.

"My brother used to have a reputation for drinking more than anyone else. He would come home in a right state sometimes, but one night he didn't come home at all. Mum was out of her mind with worry, and almost broke down when a call came through from the hospital. It turned out he had got so plastered that he passed out and cracked his head on the pavement. He doesn't drink so much nowadays."

Alexia (13)

Drink to get drunk and the end result is always the same. If you're lucky, you'll escape with a bad hangover. Then again, you could wind up puking into a toilet bowl, wishing the world would stop spinning around you, or worse. What with the increased risks of accidents, violence and doing things you badly regret, abusing alcohol can come at a high price.

BOOZE BULLETIN

Alcohol is believed to feature as a reason for a quarter of all school exclusions in the UK.

OTHER REASONS FOR DRINKING

The desire for fun and excitement may be uppermost in people's minds when they drink. Others turn to alcohol because they feel it helps them deal with certain situations. However, there can be other factors beyond the immediate effects that you may not be aware of at the time, but which can lead to long term problems:

Drinking and sex

Drinking might make you feel braver (which is sometimes known as 'Dutch courage') but it also increases the chances of taking risks you might regret. Sure, alcohol lowers inhibitions, but in some ways your guard is up for good reason when you're sober. Getting physically intimate with someone is a big step at any time, and it's bound to make you feel nervous. Fuelling your desires with drink might appear to ease your nerves, but all you're really doing is losing control over the situation. As a result, you're less likely to enjoy the experience and feel good about yourself afterwards. You also stand a greater risk of forgetting to take precautions against pregnancy or sexually transmitted infections. At worst, it can cause you to be the victim of a sexual assault. Ultimately drunken sex is a recipe for disaster. Check out a recent survey of 14-16 year-olds. The statistics speak for themselves:

- One in seven admitted to having unprotected sex while drunk.
- One in five regretted having sex after getting drunk.
- 10% claimed they couldn't remember if they'd even had sex because they were so drunk at the time.

"I lost my virginity when I was drunk, but it's not something I'm very proud about. The guy just wanted sex, because he lost interest in me afterwards. I'm sure I would've sussed him out and stopped had I been sober."

Cathy (16)

If you're female and you've had drunken sex without condoms, or suspect you've slept with someone but can't be sure, don't just pretend it never happened. You can't ignore the risk of pregnancy. To be effective, the morning-after pill has to be taken within 72 hours of unprotected sex, so visit your doctor or a health clinic as soon as possible. At the same time they can check for infection, and offer the right treatment.

"It's a real turn off when a lad's been drinking and he tries to chat you up."

Siri (15)

BOOZE BULLETIN

Lads may find themselves unable to get an erection while drunk. Alcohol is known to cause impotence, which is sometimes called 'brewer's droop'. So even if sex is on the cards, you may find getting plastered could lead to an embarrassing let-down in more ways than one.

Drinking and boredom

All too often, people feel they have nothing better to do than get drunk. Like any drug, it offers a short-term escape from their everyday lives but what it doesn't offer is a solution to the problem. If you think life's dull, drink isn't going to make it any better. If anything, it'll sap your self-esteem and increase your risk of getting into trouble for anti-social behaviour.

"I was drinking in this car park, killing time with a couple of mates, when one of them dared me to go roof walking over a line of cars. It seemed like a laugh, and I was so out of it I didn't think about the fact that we were being watched on a closed-circuit camera. I'm still waiting to hear if I'll go to court, but even if the charges are dropped it's going to take time for my dad to calm down."

Dean (16)

Drinking and stress

From exams to peer pressure, family life to love issues, all manner of things can leave us feeling tense and irritable. The key is to understand what's causing you to feel so stressed, and find ways to make it work for you. Talking about the issue, taking exercise or teaching yourself to relax can work wonders. All too often, however, the temptation is to escape from stress. Alcohol might numb your anxieties, but it's no solution. If anything, you sober up to find your problems have grown.

"I was dreading my exams last year. Every time I sat down to revise I freaked out about failing, and found it hard to concentrate. Sometimes I would sneak a couple of my dad's beers from the fridge, and drink them upstairs. It helped me chill a bit while I worked, but I didn't take anything in."

Mike (15)

Drinking as a way of life

Anyone can develop dependency problems with alcohol. There can be many complex reasons for this, ranging from your family's relationship with drink, your social scene and your state of mind, but the bottom line is this: if you feel compelled to drink to feel normal, or to escape from certain issues in your life, then you have a problem that needs addressing.

"Once I was on a course of medicine, which meant I couldn't drink. I went to a party that weekend, and felt weird about being sober. I just didn't enjoy myself, and that worried me."

Petra (15)

Alcoholism is considered to be a disease. The term applies to someone who feels compelled to drink, despite being aware of the physical, mental and social harm it's causing them. In other words, that person has lost control to drink. Some medical professionals prefer not to use this term, however, as they believe many people with drink dependency problems don't think of themselves as alcoholics, and as a result they're less likely to tackle the issue.

"I know I drink a lot, but I'm not an alcoholic."

Holly (15)

When people talk about alcoholics, it's easy to conjure up an image of someone sprawled in a gutter clutching an empty bottle. The reality is very different, however. Some people are able to confine their drinking habit to a particular time of day (the evening, for example) while people who booze heavily on a regular basis may become so tolerant of alcohol that it's hard to tell that they've even been drinking.

BOOZE BULLETIN

A 'binge drinker' is a term used to describe someone who can go for long periods without drinking, and then hit the bottle in a big way – often boozing for days at a time. Even though they're able to do without alcohol for some time, it's still classed as a serious problem, particularly among young drinkers.

MYTHS ABOUT DRINK AND DRINKERS

"Alcohol gives you energy."

The truth: alcohol is a depressant drug. It actually slows down your body system.

"Beer is less harmful than spirits like whisky."

The truth: a drink like whisky may contain more alcohol by volume, but beer can cause just as much damage if you consume enough of it.

"Drugs are a bigger problem than alcohol."

The truth: alcohol is classified as a drug, just like substances such as cannabis, tobacco, heroin and cocaine. Twice as many people are dependent on alcohol as on all other forms of legal and illegal drugs.

"It's OK to get hammered, so long as you don't do it all the time."

The truth: drinking large amounts of alcohol can be very dangerous at any time, but especially if your body's not used to alcohol.

"An alcoholic is always drunk."

The truth: drink dependency problems affect people of all ages, from all walks of life, but each one has a unique relationship with alcohol. Some can go for long periods without touching a drop, while others find it impossible to function without it.

ALL ABOUT ALCOPOPS

What are they?

Generally speaking, alcopops are fizzy drinks that contain alcohol (i.e. alcoholic lemonade, milkshakes and fruit flavoured wines). They tend to be brightly coloured, with a high sugar content and street-smart names. Alcopops often contain more alcohol by volume than many popular lagers and ciders.

Who drinks them?

The manufacturers maintain that alcopops are designed to appeal to the 18-25 market. However there is some concern that much younger people are drawn to the image surrounding these drinks, and the fact that they taste so sweet.

Why the concern?

Research has shown that young people are more likely to drink large amounts in single sessions. It may be tempting to consume alcopops, but the alcohol content behind that sugary taste can mean you end up getting more drunk than expected – often with unpleasant results. Bleurchhh!

CHAPTER THREE

The impact of alcohol

"A couple of days after a heavy drinking session,
I often break out in spots!"

Sean (15)

"I've had some good times with drink and some bad
times too. There's nothing worse than getting to the
point where you know you're going to be sick."

Andrea (14)

"I saw a TV documentary about some rock star who
became an alcoholic. He looked completely burned
out, and spoke like his brain wasn't functioning
properly."

Connor (13)

It's easy to think that the effects of a night out
boozing stop with a hangover. The fact is alcohol
has an impact on your health, not just on your body
but also your mind. Here's what can happen if you
keep on overdoing the drink.

YOUR SKIN

Boozing can muck up your skin on two counts. Not only does it mess with your metabolism, depriving the skin of vital nutrients, but it also leaves you dehydrated (lacking water). The result? Your skin loses its elasticity, and becomes prone to spots and early wrinkles. Long-term alcohol abuse may also lead to broken blood vessels just below the surface of the skin, which can leave you with a ruddy complexion.

"If I get really drunk, I always feel clammy for a day afterwards."

Curtis (15)

BOOZE BULLETIN

Alcohol depletes your body of vitamin B complex. A lack of this vital nutrient can result in skin damage, diarrhoea and even depression.

YOUR STOMACH AND LIVER

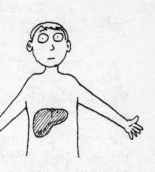

OK, so it's not as glamorous as the heart, and poets rarely wax lyrical about its properties. Even so, your liver is the largest single organ in the body, and deals with the blood that flows from the intestinal tract to your ticker.

When you drink, your liver works overtime to metabolise the alcohol. Like any engine, however, the more you thrash it the greater the risk of it breaking down. In this case, a heavy duty drinking habit leaves you prone to stomach bleeding, fatty liver, alcoholic hepatitis and a condition called cirrhosis. It's here that the cells in your liver gradually give up the ghost and turn to scar tissue, which prevents it from functioning properly. There is no cure for cirrhosis. It is linked to cancer of the liver, and can even prove to be fatal.

"A friend of my dad has cirrhosis of the liver and he looks like death warmed up. He's horribly thin and his skin is really yellow. My dad says he doesn't drink now because his doctor warned that any more could kill him."

Iain (15)

Warning signs of cirrhosis include jaundice (yellowing of the skin and whites of the eyes) and a build up of fluid in the abdomen. Some cases have been reported of cirrhosis in men as young as 19-20 who started drinking heavily in their early teens.

WEIGHT AND DIET

Alcohol might be virtually fat free, but the same can't be said for an alcoholic drink. Why? Because booze is either grain-based and high in starch (lager, bitter), or fruit-based and high in sugar content (wine). Check out the average calorific content of some typical drinks:

Pint of bitter:	200 calories
Pint of lager:	170 calories
Glass of red wine:	90 calories
Glass of champagne:	80 calories
Measure of whisky:	55 calories

It may not sound like much, but a couple of pints in the evening could add almost a quarter to your recommended daily calorie intake. Studies also show that there is no significant nutritional value in an alcoholic drink. It just provides empty calories that can quickly end up on your waistline, or leave you malnourished if you're fooled into thinking drink has a place in your diet.

"I decided to stop drinking because I was worried about my weight and I'd heard that lager can be really fattening. Within a month, I'd lost a couple of pounds. Ever since then I think of drink like junk food - it's nice as a treat, but it won't do my health any favours if I have too much!"

Amanda (15)

BOOZE BULLETIN

A beer gut, or beer belly, is a term used to describe a build up of fat in and around the abdominal area. Up to 40% of all blokes are likely to blob out here, and it's almost certainly fuelled by a couch potato lifestyle that involves boozing on a regular basis.

YOUR HEART

As an adult, your ticker won't be tortured by moderate drinking. But if you're boozing on a bigger scale you run an increased risk of high blood pressure, heart attacks and heart disease.

"I like to go jogging every day, but if I've been out the night before I can't get half way round the park without my heart trying to kick its way out of my chest!"

Damien (15)

YOUR BRAIN

Drinking destroys brain cells, which means a heavy long-term habit can result in brain shrinkage and nerve damage. Some experts also think that heavy, regular boozing in your teenage years can affect brain development involved in learning and memory.

"Sometimes I wake up after a big night out, and it feels like I've got a stone rattling round inside my head instead of a brain."

Marcus (16)

BOOZE BULLETIN

Wernicke-Korsakoff syndrome is a brain disorder closely linked to alcoholism. Symptoms include amnesia, loss of short-term memory, hallucinations, emotional disturbances and loss of muscle control.

MENTAL HEALTH

It's not just your body that bears the brunt of booze abuse. Drinking slows down your nervous system, which means it can affect your mental state in both the short and long term. Irritability and memory loss can be a factor the morning after a big night out, as can a reduced sex drive.

> "If my sister's been out drinking the night before, we all know she'll be seriously grumpy until lunchtime. Even her boyfriend keeps his distance!"
>
> Rachel (14)

Alcohol is also closely related to depression, and if you're prone to feeling blue then booze will only make things worse. In fact it's estimated that alcohol has been involved in about 65% of all suicide attempts in the UK.

> "My mum drank more when she was going through the divorce. Sometimes I'd find her crying at the kitchen table with a glass in front of her and a half finished bottle of wine."
>
> Tina (13)

DEPENDENCY PROBLEMS

Someone who drinks a lot on a regular basis runs a high risk of becoming alcohol dependent. As their tolerance develops, so they need to drink more in order to feel the effects.

Eventually, their mind and body get so used to the presence of alcohol that they need to drink to feel normal (psychological dependence), and to avoid some unpleasant and sometimes dangerous withdrawal symptoms (physical dependence).

"My dad says his brother was a different person before he started drinking. Nowadays things have got so bad it seems to me he only lives to get drunk. It's really tragic."

Daniel (13)

Nobody sets out to become an alcoholic. It's something that can creep up on a drinker over a period of time, often without them realising or accepting that there is a problem. The bottom line is this: if drink plays such an important role in your life that you'd find it hard to manage without, then you need to address the underlying reasons before things get out of hand.

WITHDRAWAL SYMPTOMS

In some ways, a hangover is evidence that your body is withdrawing from the toxic effects of alcohol. For someone who is chronically dependent on alcohol, however, the withdrawal symptoms can amount to far more than a pain behind the eyes and a desire to lie down all day. Without proper medical care, in fact, the detoxification experience could actually be fatal.

"My mum's a nurse, and one day she took my brother and I to a centre where they treat alcoholics. The doctor told us that most of the patients were on medication to help them break their drinking habits. He said if they just stopped boozing without proper care, their bodies would go into shock and some of these people could be dead within a week. Believe me, the pair of us looked at drink in a different light after that little visit!"

Ben (13)

Delirium Tremens (DT's)

This is a disturbance of the brain that affects some alcoholics, and can kick in between 12-48 hours after that person stops drinking, i.e. after a night's sleep. This is why the shakes they may experience are most apparent in the morning.

"My grandfather was an alcoholic. He used to come downstairs for breakfast and pretend everything was fine, but he couldn't hide the fact that his hands were shaking. Then he'd head off to his allotment for a couple of hours, and everyone knew he'd gone drinking because when he came back he was always a little steadier."

Ryan (13)

Other symptoms of the DT's can include sleep disorders such as insomnia, hallucinations, disorientation, convulsions, epileptic seizures of the *grand mal* type, anxiety and fear, agitation, fast pulse, fever, extreme perspiration. In some cases, it can even lead to coma and death.

Physically withdrawing from a serious long-term alcohol habit can take anything between one and ten days. But in some ways it's only the start of the road to recovery. As we'll see later on, the biggest challenge for anyone with a drink dependency problem is finding a way to stay sober.

REAL LIFE

Drinking before a date was a regular event for **Daisy, 15, until a few home truths changed her attitude to alcohol.**

It became a bit of a ritual, drinking on the sly while I got ready to go out with Guy. I never got totally smashed, but I'm naturally shy and needed something to help me relax. I used to buy little bottles of ready mixed rum and coke from a shop where the owner never asked questions, and swig it in my bedroom. One was enough for a while, but sometimes I'd got through two before leaving my house.

Dutch courage

I'd always fancied Guy, and was thrilled when we got together. A lot of my mates were really envious, and I didn't want to lose him. That's why I felt it was so important to make a good impression, and having a drink seemed the best way to help me do this. Usually we would meet in town, and I'd just burble away about everything and anything until he was laughing along with me. I never mentioned the drink, basically because I wanted him to think I was always this outgoing.

Something to hide

I quickly found myself falling for Guy, though I did worry that he was holding something back from me. He could go very quiet at times, especially if I got an attack of the giggles (which I often did if I was tipsy). But the one thing that troubled me most was the fact that Guy never took me back to his house. He'd been over to mine many times, but there was always some reason why I couldn't visit him. "My grandma's staying," he would say. Or, "we've got the builders in." At first I didn't think anything of it, but the longer it went on, the more I started to think he had something to hide. Eventually, my curiosity got the better of me and I pitched up at his house unannounced. "Daisy!" he seemed surprised to see me, and slightly panicked too. "Well," I said, "aren't you going to ask me in?"

The secret's out

Guy's mum was lovely. Really sweet and kind. She offered to make a cup of tea, and I was just wondering why he had been so reluctant for me to visit when his dad came into the room. He didn't say anything, but his presence put all three of us on edge. He was thin as a rake, and just looked ill. He said hello, and I noticed his hand was trembling as I shook it. Then he just stood there, looking slightly lost. I was deeply relieved when Guy suggested we go out.

Drink rethink

Guy's dad was an alcoholic. It was something Guy had learned to live with over the years, but which had clearly affected his family. They obviously cared for him, but Guy said it was like living with someone who was just falling apart in front of them. He said his Mum had tried to leave a number of times, but came back because his dad couldn't cope. Then he said something that left me cold. He asked me if I always drank before a date. I went bright red, spluttered something about wanting to have a good time, and wished the ground would swallow me up.

Fresh start

I'm still seeing Guy, and we're much closer since that day. I don't go round to his house much, because I know how uncomfortable it makes him. I also don't drink any more before we go out. I haven't given up altogether, but booze no longer has a place in our relationship, and we're both better off as a result.

CHAPTER FOUR

Other risks

"Towards the end of a party recently, my best mate's girlfriend sat down on my lap. We were both out of it, and just chatting, but then suddenly she kissed me and I didn't stop her. The next thing I knew my mate appeared in front of us, demanding to know what was going on. Drink basically destroyed my friendship. What a waste!"

Ryan (15)

"I don't drink much if I'm at a family gathering, because I know I'll only do or say something I might regret."

Shane (16)

"A boy from my school was killed by a drunk driver. The guy behind the wheel was only 17. Can you imagine living with something like that?"

Steph (14)

IMPOTENCE AND INFERTILITY

A guy's penis might appear to have a life of its own, but his ability to get an erection is actually down to the brain in his head.

Drinking may boost his confidence up there, but it also serves to dull the sensory nerve transmissions between his bonce and the contents of his boxer shorts. The result? Even a pint can affect his performance, and stop him from achieving maximum erection potential. Hence the term 'brewer's droop'!

"If a lad wants to chat me up, he'd better be sober. There's nothing worse than having a drunk who thinks he's God's gift to women slobber all over you!"

Claire (15)

What's more, heavy long term boozing can lead to more permanent problems in the trouser department such as reduced testosterone levels and an increased risk of infertility.

PREGNANCY

Alcohol and pregnancy don't mix well. There's a great deal of concern about the effect of alcohol on the unborn child, basically because it can easily cross the placenta. This means if the mother has a drink then the foetus gets a dose too, at a time of critical brain development.

"I once saw a woman who was pregnant and drunk. It was a tragic sight, and one I won't forget for a long time to come."

Ruth (14)

Experts reckon pregnant women who drink six or more units of alcohol a day may give birth to babies affected by a condition known as Foetal Alcohol syndrome. Symptoms can include:

- smaller heads and brains
- abnormal facial features (small upper lip, nose and jaw, contracted eyelids)
- mental retardation
- poor coordination
- hyperactivity
- malformation of the heart, external genital organs and joints.

There is also evidence to suggest that pregnant women drinking smaller amounts may result in a baby being born with a low birth weight.

BOOZE BULLETIN

Due to hormone level changes, a woman's reaction to alcohol may vary at different stages of her menstrual cycle. Women who take the contraceptive pill may take longer to burn off the booze in their bodies than they otherwise would.

ALCOHOL AND OTHER DRUGS

M ixing drink with any other drug is dangerous. Why? Because different drugs have different effects, but the impact of some drugs may be greatly increased when combined with alcohol. In some cases, it can kill. For example, drinking on top of other depressant drugs such as tranquillisers, sleeping pills, heroin or barbiturates can cause the central nervous system to slow down so dramatically that it shuts down brain and heart activity.

"My sister got a bit drunk at a party recently, and was having a fairly good time until someone offered her a spliff. She reckoned about a minute after her first drag she felt like keeling over, and had to go outside to be sick. Afterwards her mate said she steers clear of cannabis if she's been drinking, because it always leaves her feeling nauseous."

Beatrice (15)

BOOZE BULLETIN

Anyone taking prescription drugs, or over-the-counter medication, should not drink alcohol without first seeking advice from their GP or pharmacist.

ACCIDENTS

Alcohol is known to impair judgement, which means people are more likely to take risks if they've been boozing. Your balance and coordination are also badly compromised, as is your ability to respond to danger. In fact it's estimated that up to one third of all accidents, at home and work, are drink related.

"I was messing around with my mates in town, spraying lager from our cans and shoving each other around. I remember my mate Dan getting pushed, but he tripped and went straight through the glass front of our local chemist. He ended up with seventy stitches in his hands and face."

Finn (15)

BOOZE BULLETIN

Swimming 'under the influence' can be very dangerous, particularly in cold water because alcohol creates a false sense of warmth. This can lead to hyperventilation and cardiovascular collapse. 15% of all cases of drowning in the UK are alcohol-related.

ALCOHOL AND CRIME

Drinking doesn't make people break the law, but it is closely associated with criminal behaviour. Recent research suggests that 88% of criminal damage,

78% of assaults and 40% of violent crime cases are committed while the offender is under the influence of alcohol. Being drunk and disorderly in a public place is an offence in its own right, and in recent years the government has taken steps to 'call time' on the drunken thugs.

"There used to be a pub nearby where it was easy to get served. It was also a hotspot for violence on a Friday night. Anyone with a brain used to avoid the place at closing time, because people would always come out looking for trouble. Finally the police raided the place. Loads of people I know got caught up in it. Soon after, the landlord lost his licence."

Jade (15)

The relationship between boozing and breaking the law is complex, but the fact is you're more likely to be involved in trouble if drink is around. Nowhere is this more apparent than in cases of violent crime and road accidents.

BOOZE BULLETIN

Almost half the incidents of disorderly behaviour dealt with by the police happen around pub closing time.

Road accidents

It's not just drunk drivers who put themselves at risk when they hit the road. Statistically speaking, both passengers and pedestrians are almost twice as likely to be injured or killed in drink-related car accidents. Every year in the UK, over five hundred people lose their lives in this way. Nowadays most people agree that drink driving is antisocial and reckless, yet despite public campaigns and police crackdowns the number of accidents has started to climb.

"My dad is OK about me drinking, providing I don't go too over the top. What worries him is drink-driving, but I'm with him on that one – there's no way I would get in a car with anyone who's been near alcohol."

Sal (14)

The legal limit for driving in the UK is 80 mg of alcohol per 100 ml of blood. The number of drinks it takes to reach this level varies from person to person, but ultimately safety experts advise people not to drink at all if they are going to drive. It clouds your judgement, co-ordination, thought processes and concentration – all the things you need to get from A to B without harming yourself or anyone else.

According to the Road Traffic Act 1988, the police can ask someone to be tested if they have reasonable cause to suspect that:

- the person has been driving (or attempting to drive) with alcohol in their body

- a moving-traffic offence has been committed
- the person has been involved in an accident.

The police have the right to test the suspect's breath, blood or urine, and they can be charged if the following levels are exceeded:

- 35 milligrams of alcohol in 100 millilitres of breath
- 107 milligrams of alcohol per 100 millilitres of urine
- 80 milligrams of alcohol in 100 millilitres of blood.

It's worth bearing in mind that the body burns up alcohol at a rate of one unit per hour. This could mean that someone who's had a heavy night drinking might still be 'under the influence' the next morning. They may think they are fit to drive, but alcohol could still be present in their system. If in doubt don't accept a lift. It might be a hassle trying to find an alternative means of transport, but at least you can be sure you'll get there in one piece.

Finally, if you're going to drink, be smart about heading places on foot. Recent statistics reveal that 37% of pedestrians killed on the roads have drunk over the legal limit for driving.

BOOZE BULLETIN

Almost 20% of all drivers killed in road crashes are under the influence of drugs other than alcohol. In general terms, smoking one cannabis joint is the equivalent of being just over the legal limit.

Violence

Boozing can bring out a bad side in some people, especially when it comes to violence. Why? Because alcohol disrupts an area of brain function that deals with the ability to restrain impulses. It also stokes up your confidence and messes with your ability to assess the risk of acting violently. All this boils down to the fact that if you get drunk and flirt with the idea of a fight, you're likely to end up on a losing streak!

"My ex-boyfriend used to go drinking in this pub that had a reputation for violence. I think he reckoned it was cool, but more often than not he'd end up making a swift getaway or risk getting his head kicked in!"

Emma (15)

Not everyone has a tendency to turn nasty when they're drunk. In fact many people become positively weepy after a couple of drinks! Even so, research shows that a high proportion of victims of violent crime are drinking or under the influence of alcohol at the time of their assault.

REAL LIFE

Jim, 18, was the victim of a drunken attack that left him scarred both physically and mentally. He relives the experience here.

I'd arranged to meet a mate on a Friday night. Nothing heavy. Just a pint with an old friend I hadn't seen for a while. We were in my local pub at the time, chatting about the people we still kept in touch with. It was busy, and we couldn't get a seat, which meant people who were trying to get to the bar were constantly jostling us. Eventually we decided to find somewhere quieter, but opted to get one more drink while we thought about the best place to go. If we had left then, I would've avoided the most terrifying event in my whole life.

Flash point

My mate went off to get a couple of pints, and I just hung back to wait for him. I watched him slide his way through the crush, only to be stopped midway by this stocky guy with a beer bottle in his paw and trouble written all over his face.

"Pick another route, pal. It's rude to push."

My mate raised his palms, and tried to slide by, but the next thing I knew the guy had shoved him back a step. I could see he was trying to provoke a fight, and quickly moved in to see if I could calm things down.

"Come on, mate," I reasoned. "We don't need this."

He was shorter than me, but sized me up like he was calling the shots. My heart was hammering, and a fight was the last thing I needed. I'm not a violent person by any stretch, and was deeply relieved when the guy backed down. He didn't say a word. Just grinned and raised the bottle as if to salute me. I nodded back, dismissing him as another dumb drunk, and retreated with my mate to the bar. As far as I was concerned, it was just one of those stupid confrontations that finish as quickly as they start. I rested my elbows on the bar, feeling a little shaken up, and the next thing I know I felt this shattering crack to the back of my head.

Attack

There was a stunned silence, and then panic broke out. I wheeled around, but my legs gave way underneath me. I remember the guy getting pulled away, and a warm sticky feeling in my hair. It was blood. Lots of it. The guy had hit me so hard with his bottle that it had shattered on impact. Mercifully, I passed out at this point, because it turned out that a shard of glass had been driven deep into my neck and sliced a main artery. It was the landlord who saved my life. He used bar towels to staunch the bleeding while an ambulance raced to the scene. I ended up with dozens of stitches in my neck, and it's left some nasty scars.

Aftermath

The whole episode left me feeling depressed for months. It was so pointless. So dumb. The guy responsible got fined, but that was all. I'm told that at the court hearing he claimed he acted out of character because he was drunk. In some ways that was more of an insult to me than the punishment he received. It really changed my outlook on alcohol. I still drink, but I'm wary of blokes who have been boozing. To me, they're potentially dangerous weapons.

BOOZE BULLETIN

Every week in the UK, 13,000 violent incidents take place in or near licensed premises such as pubs, bars and off licences. Drunken violence is also responsible for some 76,000 facial injuries each year.

Problem pages overleaf →

DRINK AND EXERCISE

I live in a rural part of the country, and often walk home after parties. I'm reasonably fit, and normally I can do it without breaking sweat, but if I've been boozing it leaves me feeling flushed and exhausted. Is this down to the drink?

Gary (15)

Booze could well be behind these symptoms. Here's how:

Tiredness: Alcohol is a diuretic, which means it encourages the body to lose water (by making you pee more). Bizarre as it sounds, the more alcohol you drink, the thirstier you become. As a result, you could well be dehydrated when you begin your hike home, and tiredness is a major symptom.

Flushes: This is a sign that your cooling system isn't working at full speed, which is another sign of alcohol-related dehydration. Any form of physical exercise will raise your body temperature. Normally, this triggers the sweating mechanism to keep you cool. If your body is deprived of water, however, it affects your ability to perspire. As a result you're left with flushed skin and even an uncomfortable prickly sensation.

Walking 'under the influence' also places you at greater risk of accidents. You're less alert, and your responses are dumbed down too. So if you want to stay safe when you leave the party and hit the country lanes, stay hydrated and pack a torch or, better still, get a taxi home!

BOOZE BLACKOUTS

The last few times I've got myself really blasted, I've woken up with absolutely no idea where I've been or what I said or did. What's going on here?

Kaj (15)

It sounds like you've experienced alcohol-related blackouts. These are basically periods of amnesia, or memory loss, which can kick in when alcohol affects the part of the brain that deals with memory formation. A blackout isn't the same as passing out, which is basically a loss of consciousness, but it should be viewed as a wake-up call to the fact that you're drinking too much.

Not only is it a sign that you're abusing your body with booze, blacking out has serious implications regarding your personal safety and the safety of others. If you can't recall what you did, then chances are you had little control over the situation. It's a scary thought, because you're responsible for your actions no matter what state you're in, so hopefully it should encourage you to review your relationship with alcohol.

If you find it hard to cut down, or control your drinking habit, then consult your GP, or get further support and advice from Drinkline (see Contacts at the end of the book).

CHAPTER FIVE

Dealing with drink

"A couple of ciders can bring out a whole different side in me. Sometimes it's lots of fun, but there have been occasions where I've drunk too much and regretted it badly."

Adele (15)

"Drinking on an empty stomach might mean I get blasted quicker, but with nothing to mop up the booze there's always the risk that I end up feeling giddy and sick."

Dean (15)

"The best way to avoid a hangover? Don't drink in the first place!"

Bobby (14)

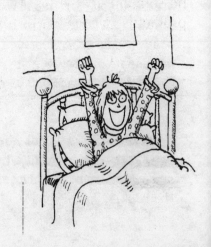

CHOOSE NOT TO BOOZE?

Alcohol isn't to everyone's taste. It's not something you should ever feel obliged to do, because if you're relying on drink for a good time then you're drinking for all the wrong reasons. Despite the fact that boozing plays such a big part in our culture, never lose sight of the fact that it always remains a choice. You don't have to drink or get drunk to enjoy yourself, as many non-drinkers will tell you:

"I used to be a big boozer, but one day I woke up with the mother of all hangovers and decided to see if I could go without. Staying sober at parties was weird to begin with, but it actually helped me become a lot more confident as a person. I still go out as much as I used to, but I actually think I enjoy myself more."

Stephen (16)

"Alcohol just doesn't appeal to me. I'm quite happy to go out with people who drink, providing they don't get completely blitzed. Nobody treats me any differently, and if they do it says more about their attitude to drink than it does about me."

Alison (15)

"Every other weekend, I deliberately steer clear of drinking. It's my way of reminding myself that I can go without."

Sean (15)

If you are partial to a pint, or you like a drink when you're out with your mates, why not try and go without? Just for once? It may seem like a simple request, and chances are it won't cause you any difficulties. At the very least, however, it will encourage you to think about what role alcohol plays in your life, and that can only be a good thing. Here are ten ways to duck out of the next drink:

- "I have to be up first thing in the morning."
- "I feel a cold coming on."
- "I don't drink one day a week, and it's this one."
- "I'm still hung over from the last time we went out!"
- "I'm all out of cash."

- "I'm taking a reality check."
- "I don't mix alcohol with pleasure."
- "My body is a temple, not a back street boozer."
- "I'm grumpy when I'm drunk."
- "Why bother? We're already having fun!"

BOOZE BULLETIN

Despite the rise in alcohol use and abuse among young people, about 40% of 11-15 year olds in Britain do not drink.

THINK BEFORE YOU DRINK

To drink, or not to drink? The decision is down to you. You're aware of the risks, but perhaps you also feel that with a little respect it can be fun sometimes. That's why being smart about alcohol means thinking ahead. Here are some tips to help make sure booze doesn't get the better of you:

- **Eat a decent meal** before you go out. Stuff like bread, potatoes and pasta, and fatty food such as chips, take a while to digest and will help absorb alcohol.
- **Know your limits.** Don't set out to drink up to the amount of alcohol your body can tolerate. Instead, aim to enjoy a drink as part of that social setting, but be careful not to exceed your limits. If you're not sure what you can handle, however, then take it very easy indeed.

- **Pace yourself.** Give your body a chance to process the alcohol from one drink to the next. Also sip each drink instead of swigging it down. It'll give you greater control, and reduce the risk of embarrassing yourself in front of everyone.
- **Alternate alcohol with water.** Keep up the fluids that matter by switching to a non-alcoholic, non-fizzy drink every now and then.
- **Avoid mixing drinks.** Your body won't thank you for sending down different types of booze. It means more toxins to deal with, while the different alcohol levels can make it harder for you to hold that line between enjoying yourself and wishing you hadn't had that last drink.

BOOZE BULLETIN

According to recent reports, nearly half of all British teenagers know how to buy bootlegged beer that has been smuggled illegally into the country.

DRINKING AT HOME

For many families, alcohol is something nobody talks about. Like sex and drugs, it's an issue some parents in particular may feel unable or unwilling to discuss openly. The trouble with steering clear of the subject is that it creates a taboo. With their curiosity rising, and no one else to turn to for advice, many young people find their own answers by taking silly risks on their own terms.

If your folks enjoy the odd drink, however, and you feel comfortable raising the issue, why not go ahead and ask them about it? OK, so they're unlikely to let you drink freely around the house, but they may provide a controlled environment for you to see what all the fuss is about.

"If we're eating together, my dad sometimes asks if I'd like a glass of wine. It's cool because it means I've never been afraid to ask him questions about alcohol."

Calista (15)

Ultimately, the more open you can be about alcohol with your parents the better. It might be tempting to just help yourself to their drinks cabinet when there's nobody at home, but learning about booze by your mistakes just doesn't match up to learning from people you trust. If a parent or carer is prepared to supervise your early experiences of drink, it means you get to satisfy your curiosity without taking any needless risks.

Plus you break the ice about booze, which can only make it easier for you to raise questions in future.

"I expected to get grounded when my dad found out I'd been nicking his beers. Instead he blamed himself for not talking to me about drink, which made me feel even more uncomfortable. But since then things have been much better between us. He knows I drink at parties now. His only concern is that I don't go too far, and also that I understand why!"

Will (14)

DRINKING ALONE

Many young people first try a taste of alcohol when they're alone. It's easy to see why. You don't want to be seen to know nothing, but you're curious to see what it's like. At the same time you do run very serious risks if the effects take you by surprise and there's nobody around to help.

"When I was nine, I found a tumbler of whisky that my dad hadn't finished. I forced myself to drink it. I don't think I had any idea how I would feel, but I wanted to find out, and it really scared me when my head started spinning. I tried to keep away from my mum when she got home, but she smelled the drink on my breath. The first thing she did was help me sober up, and when my dad came home she burst into tears. Which meant I felt bad for two reasons."

Nicole (13)

BOOZE BULLETIN

Alcohol Concern report that by the end of the 90's the average weekly amount drunk by all 11-15 year-olds was 1.6 alcohol units, compared with 0.8 units at the beginning of that decade.

Experimenting with alcohol in secret is one thing, but drinking alone on a regular basis suggests you may be trying to drown certain feelings relating to troubling issues in your life. Anything from stress to depression can persuade people to hit the bottle, but it's no solution to the problem. Tips for cutting down or breaking free from drink dependency problems can be found in Chapter Six.

"Revising for exams has always freaked me out, and when a mate suggested a drink would help me to relax I stupidly gave it a go. Sure, a couple of cans calmed my nerves, but I might as well have been looking at blank pages! Every time I tried to focus, my thoughts swam somewhere else."

Lewis (15)

BOOZE BULLETIN

Neolithic Man is the earliest known drinker, having consumed berry wine in 6400 BC!

OUT AND ABOUT WITH ALCOHOL

No matter what room there is for alcohol in your home environment, it's bound to be a feature in your social life. Even those who choose not to drink would be hard pressed to find themselves at a booze-free club, gathering or party. At times like this, it's easy to get carried away with the moment and drink more than you can handle.

"This girl I really fancied was waiting for me to make a move at a party once. A friend suggested I take a couple of swigs of vodka before I talked to her. I've never drunk anything so quickly, and it went straight to my head. As a result, I managed to break the ice, but I started feeling giddy soon after and had to sit down with my head between my knees. In the end, she got off with someone else!"

Kieran (15)

Thinking about the consequences of downing a drink can only help minimise the risks. Next time you're faced with a situation where alcohol is an option, just stop to ask how it'll leave you feeling. Have you eaten recently to help you cope with the booze in your body? Will you need a straight head in the next few hours? Do you know what strength this drink is, and have you experienced it before? It may sound like a lot to go through, but steaming in and getting sozzled for the sake of it can only bring you grief.

"Everyone tends to fool about with drinking to begin with, but then nobody likes throwing up all over themselves. Eventually, you have to wise up to the fact that booze is something to be respected. Otherwise you're just asking for trouble."

Megan (15)

BOOZE BULLETIN

Young people experience comas at lower blood alcohol levels, which is why experimental drinking can be so dangerous. In 1996, one UK casualty department treated two hundred 9 to 16 year olds who were under the influence of alcohol; many needed resuscitation from a large overdose. Most had drunk vodka or strong cider.

ALCOHOL AND SPECIAL OCCASIONS

Booze has been used to mark big events for centuries. Whether you're wetting a baby's head or attending a funeral wake, alcohol features from the moment the doors open on our lives right through to closing time! At a time when you're just beginning to get to grips with alcohol, a family event such as an engagement or a birthday party might seem like an ideal drinking opportunity. But before you knock back the champagne, stop to think about the consequences of losing your head at a time like this.

> *"I got so plastered at my sister's wedding that I finished the evening curled up in the corner of the marquee! My dad didn't think it was so funny, and made me get up early the next morning to clear up the mess. I felt really ill, but he told me that was no excuse."*
>
> **Christopher (15)**

Being drunk and disorderly is one thing if you're with your mates. In the presence of Auntie Patty and Uncle Bob, however, you run the risk of seriously embarrassing yourself. In some families, it's almost traditional to find yourself constantly reminded of the time you went too far. All it takes is one drink too many, but if you're sussed from the start you could earn their trust and respect instead.

"My family threw a party for my brother when he graduated from university. My grandpa kept trying to fill my glass, but I knew I'd had enough. Afterwards, he told my mum that I had a good head on my shoulders. As a result, my folks relaxed a lot more about me drinking at parties and stuff."

Alex (15)

BOOZE BULLETIN

Drop a raisin into a glass of champagne and it will repeatedly fall to the bottom and rise to the surface!

DEALING WITH HANGOVERS

Being drunk might be a buzz, but even if you're switched on about alcohol it's very hard to avoid the downside – the moment when you stop feeling good and start feeling very grim indeed.

> "A bad hangover can leave you feeling like death warmed up. You hear people going on about how much they can drink, but you never hear them boasting about how sick they felt the next day."
>
> **Luke (15)**

Nobody likes feeling hung over. The combined effects of being dehydrated by alcohol and having toxins swimming about your system can be responsible for anything from headaches and nausea to fatigue and diarrhoea. So, if you're going to drink then at least think about whether you can cope with the consequences. Boozing the night before a big exam might take your mind off things, but you're not going to perform well if you can barely focus on the paper as you turn it over!

The best way to avoid a hangover is to avoid alcohol, but if you do wake up wishing you hadn't drunk so much, here are some steps you can take to minimise the pain and suffering:

- **Keep sipping water or juice**, but avoid fizzy drinks. This is because if there's any alcohol left in your body the carbonated bubbles will stir it up!

- **Steer clear of coffee.** Many people with a hangover drink coffee because it helps them feel more alert. The trouble is that caffeine also serves to dehydrate your body further, which could leave you feeling worse.

- **Eat something.** Even though a hangover can take away your appetite, eating will help restore the glucose levels your body needs to feel good again. Stick to easily digestible stuff like toast and cereals. Even if you can't manage much, keep eating little and often.

"If I've had a few drinks the night before, I always go to bed with a glass of water because I know I'm going to wake up feeling thirsty."

Jenny (16)

It's not a good idea to take painkillers if you have a hangover. Even though they relieve headaches, the stomach lining can be quite tender after a drinking episode. As a result, you could end up adding a tummy ache to your list of troubles!

BOOZE BULLETIN

In the state of Ohio, USA, it is illegal to get a fish drunk.

Healing hangovers?

Q: Why are there so many weird and wonderful 'cures' for a hangover?

A: This is believed to be down to the fact that no matter how you choose to handle a hangover the body eventually sorts itself out. As a result, people swear by all manner of 'miracle' cures, from eating artichokes and bananas, to jogging round the park or cleaning up the house!

Unfortunately, dangerous myths are also created, such as drinking a 'hair of the dog'. This is the belief that another alcoholic drink will counteract the effects of alcohol withdrawal. In reality, all it does is stoke up the booze levels in your body. The hangover will still come back, and chances are it'll be even worse!

"My mate once cracked open a can of lager, the morning after we'd been out drinking. I could tell by the way he grimaced that he was only doing it to try and impress me. Seeing that I felt sick as a dog myself, I doubt it made him feel better."

Rory (15)

Ultimately, a hangover is a sign that you've drunk too much. There are no miracle cures. All you can do is make yourself as comfortable as you can while you bring your body back up to speed, and if a particular method works for you then go for it. While you're recovering, however, be sure to consider why you got in such a state in the first place. The more you think about drink and your motives for drinking, the less chance there is that your relationship with alcohol will slip out of control.

BOOZE BULLETIN

The Romans dealt with hangovers by eating fried canaries!

R E M E M B E R :

- Drinking is a choice. If you don't fancy it, then don't bother!
- Getting drunk doesn't guarantee a good time. That depends on the kind of person you are, where you are, and the people you're with.
- There's a fine line between enjoying a drink and letting booze control you. If you're aware of your limits, you're less likely to have a bad experience.
- If you feel able to talk about alcohol with your parent/s or carer, it can only help bring the issue into the open and establish a better understanding between you.

CHAPTER SIX

Do I have a drink problem?

"I don't drink all the time, so I'm sure I could manage without alcohol."

Max (15)

"It was only when I stopped drinking that I realised how much I had come to depend on it."

Cameron (16)

"Nobody likes to admit that booze has got the better of them. My mum only managed to cut right down when she admitted to herself that she had a problem."

Molly (13)

FACING FACTS

If you drink, then stop reading for a moment and ask how you feel about the amount you consume. Chances are you'll consider yourself to be fairly sensible about it, but the fact is a great many people who say the same actually drink far more than their weekly unit guidelines. This doesn't mean they're smashed from dawn to dusk. It just means that drink has come to play such a regular part in their lives that going without would be a problem to them.

If you're unsure whether you exceed your weekly unit allowance, try setting up a drinking diary for a while. Be sure to include every drink, the amount, the occasion, and where possible the alcohol by volume. Also make a note of whether you had a hangover and how that affected your day. That way you can build up a picture of your drinking habits, and work out whether things might be slipping out of control. Other warning signs include:

- Drinking larger amounts to get the same effect.
- Doing things when you're drunk that you later regret.
- Missing school or college because of a hangover.
- Binge drinking (going without for some time, and then drinking excessively in one period).

If you go beyond the recommended number of weekly units, or you can regularly see any of these signs in yourself, it's time to think about cutting down. If you also find you're checking off the following points, then you may well have developed a drink-dependency pattern that requires professional help.

- Boozing in secret, or hiding how much you've actually drunk.
- Thinking about alcohol a lot, and when you'll next get a chance to drink.
- Getting into trouble as a result of drink (i.e. accidents or violence).
- Finding yourself in debt because of the amount you spend on alcohol.
- Panicking when you can't get access to drink.
- Feeling the need for a drink to help cope with certain situations.
- Avoiding questions about your alcohol intake, or feeling uncomfortable about answering.
- Reacting angrily when people suggest you have a drink problem.

BOOZE BULLETIN

A study by the Office of Population and Census Surveys found that 12% of males and 7% of females in the 16-19 age group showed signs of alcohol dependence.

CUTTING DOWN AND SEEKING HELP

Nobody can force you to reduce your alcohol intake, or make you seek professional help. The only person who can take responsibility for that is you. If you've woken up to the fact that you need to cut down, here are some tips to get you started:

Look at your lifestyle

Identify those times and places when you're most likely to reach for a drink. From friends' houses, to bars or pubs with a reputation for serving underage drinkers, if you know you'll be tempted then think about steering clear. Alternatively, try turning up later than usual, to minimise your drinking time, or kick off with a soft drink to stop you feeling so thirsty.

Drink for positive reasons

Try to associate drinking with celebrations, cultural and religious events, rather than a means of blotting out your problems or propping up your self-confidence. Also think of alcohol as a complement to a fun activity with friends or family, and not just something you turn to for its own sake.

Sip it!

Binge drinking is dangerous, as your body can only process one unit of alcohol per hour. The faster you drink the more intense the effects will be, but that doesn't make the experience any more enjoyable. If you find it hard to put on the brakes, just try setting your drink down more often. If it's not in your hand all the time, you're less likely to drink it so quickly. Kick starting a conversation can also help distract you, as can something to eat (be careful with salty snacks, however, as they could just stoke your thirst).

Set yourself a limit

Before you start drinking, be sure you know when to stop. This can be hard when everyone else is boozing, but think about what goes through your head when someone offers to buy you a drink. Are you concerned about what they'll think if you say no? The fact is they won't think any less of you, and if they do then they need to review their own attitude to alcohol. So be realistic. Saying you've had enough is hard the first time, but practice makes perfect. It also avoids bad hangovers.

Take time out from drinking

If you're worried about boozing, but you don't fancy quitting completely, then set aside an alcohol-free period every now and then. Preferably one in which you would normally drink. It might be one day in a week or a month, but if you can fill that time creatively then you have nothing to lose and everything to gain.

"It was my girlfriend who first suggested I liked lager too much. At first I just laughed, but something inside me said she had a point."

Nathan (16)

Facing up to the fact that you may have a drink problem takes guts. It is perhaps the most courageous step you can take towards regaining control over your life. Help is out there too, from confidential telephone support to face-to-face counselling and more, but it's down to you to ask. Even if it's just advice you're after, or an opportunity to talk, you'll find getting the issue out into the open makes it easier to tackle. Flick to the end of the book for a list of agencies, helplines, drop-in centres and useful websites.

BOOZE BULLETIN

Low alcohol beers are brewed to taste as close to the real thing as possible, and are a popular means of keeping a drinking habit in check. They are made by stopping the fermentation process before much alcohol is produced, or by removing alcohol from regular beers using heat or vacuum distillation.

REAL LIFE

At 15, Stephen realised he needed help to control his drinking habit.

I carried the helpline number in my pocket for ages. I'd copied it from a notice board at school, but every time I came close to phoning my confidence disappeared. What made me change my mind? A throwaway comment from a friend.

Early start

I first tasted alcohol when I was 11. It was the usual story. My dad liked a drink, so it wasn't hard to steal a couple of cans of lager. I only finished half a can, however, before I decided it was a fast route to being sick, and never touched a drop for a long time after that. Even so, I remained fascinated by the whole idea of drinking, and the feeling of being drunk.

Party time!

By the time I was fourteen, most of my mates had experienced alcohol. It was appearing at parties, and that's when I really got into it. I liked getting merry on cider. So did some of my friends. It was a laugh. My dad wasn't too happy whenever he picked me up, but at the time it seemed a small price to pay.

Drinking in secret

Getting plastered with friends was one thing, but sometimes I'd have a drink alone at home. I guess I was just bored, and working out how I'd get away with it gave me something to do in the day. I was worried my dad might notice if I kept pinching cans from him, so I switched to vodka instead. I'd refill what I'd taken with water, and then drink it with lots of orange. Eventually, however, I found an off-licence where they didn't question my age, and started buying my own.

Everyone knows!

When I tell people I used to have a drink problem they assume I must've been cracking open the cans before I rolled out of bed. It wasn't really like that, though. I could go without alcohol easily, but if it was around I found it hard to resist. I didn't really give too much thought to it, but then one time I was talking with friends about different brands of lager, and one of my mates turned to me and said, "Steve, you're the only alcoholic we know. What's the best one to get you really out of your face then?" I was stunned. Stunned and embarrassed. I'd had no idea people saw me this way, even if they were only joking, and that was when I realised I had to sort myself out. I went home and promised myself I'd never drink out of line again. If only it had been that easy.

Out of hand

The next time I thought about having a drink, I had one. It was as simple as that. I kept telling myself to skip it, but I just went through the motions. Nobody was forcing me to drink, but I still did it, and I wasn't sure I liked myself much as a result.

Seeking help

I tried talking about it with my dad a couple of times, but it didn't seem right, and I knew my mum would flip if she knew. That's why I wrote down the helpline number, and began to think about calling. I was really uptight when I finally picked up the phone, but in some ways it was like talking to a friend. The woman on the other end just listened, really, and didn't make me feel bad or guilty. If anything, she gently encouraged me to think about why I was drinking, and deal with the issues in a more constructive way. I've called back a few times since then. It's good to feel I can open up about it without being yelled at or misunderstood. I haven't quit completely, but I have much more respect for alcohol and also for myself.

TEN REASONS TO CUT DOWN OR QUIT

- You're fed up with relying on booze to boost your confidence.
- You don't like regretting things you've said or done when drunk.
- You'd like to remember going to bed the night before.
- You're sick of feeling sick the next morning.
- Alcohol is calorie-packed, and you don't want to pile on the pounds.
- The cash you save could come in handy.
- You're fed up with lying to people about how much you drink.
- You'd prefer your world not to revolve around booze.
- It would be nice to say you're in control of alcohol.

CHAPTER SEVEN

Dealing with drinkers

"If I was dating a guy who got into drinking games, I wouldn't hang around to find out if he won or lost."
Gemma (16)

"My best mate can become a bit unpredictable when he's drunk. His mood can turn with little warning, and suddenly I'm in charge of Mister Angry!"
Owen (15)

herro, whatsyer name?

"People tend to talk a lot of rubbish when they're smashed."
Amelia (14)

PEER PRESSURE

It's easy to feel left out when everyone else is drinking. Whatever your reasons for staying sober, you're bound to be questioned about it. Naturally, you don't want to stand out from the crowd, and it's here that the pressure to give in can prove hard to resist.

"I only got drunk for the first time because a bottle of cider was being passed around and I didn't want to be left out."

Omar (14)

Before you go ahead and give in, just ask yourself whether boozing is going to make you a more attractive and respected person. Will your mates really think any less of you if you give it a miss this time? If anything, your determination can only invite their respect. It shows you know your mind, and that you're not prepared to let anyone dictate what you should and shouldn't do.

"I don't like alcohol, and never have done. People seem surprised when they find out, but they soon get used to it. There's always someone who will crack a joke, but if it's funny I'll laugh along too. I think if you show you're not bothered by what others think, people learn to respect you for it."

Michael (15)

BOOZE BULLETIN

On average, 21% of 11-15 year olds in the UK have had a drink in the previous week. This means more than three quarters of that age group didn't touch a drop at all!

What are friends for?

Chances are you can name one or two people you consider to be your closest friends. Sometimes it feels like you do everything together, and share both good and bad experiences. No matter what kind of bond there is between you, however, you're still an individual with a mind of your own. It may well be that you don't have the same outlook on alcohol, and that's fine. What matters is that you show the kind of respect you expect in return, and look out for them if they give you cause for concern.

"My eldest sister doesn't drink, but we still have a good time going out together. It's usually cheaper, too!"

Carol (15)

Whether you choose not to booze or you've stopped short of getting smashed, don't be intimidated if a mate gives you a hard time about it. Nobody has the right to make you feel embarrassed or uncomfortable. People do tend to behave unpredictably under the influence of alcohol, so it's easy to see how a trusted friend could suddenly turn the spotlight on you. If this happens, aim to play down the issue. Arguing with someone who's been drinking means you're unlikely to reach a sensible conclusion, but be sure to raise the issue when they're sober.

"I was playing video games at my mate's house. His mum had gone out, so we sneaked in some alcoholic lemonade. I knew I'd had enough when I found it hard to focus on the screen, but my mate made a big fuss about me not finishing my share. I really wasn't in the mood for a row, so I went home. The next day, he called to apologise for his behaviour. I really rated him for that."

Kieran (14)

BOOZE BULLETIN

The ancient Romans were the first to 'toast' special events. Nowadays, we raise our glasses or clink them together. Back then, it was done by dipping toasted bread into wine!

FRIENDS WHO DON'T DRINK

All too often, people assume that if someone doesn't drink that makes them boring. This is largely down to the fact that we live in a society where alcohol is associated with having a good time, even though the reality is often very different.

"My boyfriend doesn't drink. When we first started dating, everyone assumed it meant he was a bit square, but you only have to get to know him to realise that's rubbish!"

Eleanor (14)

In some ways, it's a bonus being mates with a non-drinker. An alcohol-free friend can make sure you don't go beyond your limit, or say things you might regret, and can even help you get home safely. Just be sure you don't take them for granted!

"I'm happy to watch out for a mate if they're the worse the wear for drink, but only because that's what being a friend is all about. If I was in trouble for a different reason, I'd expect the same help from them."

Aaron (15)

BOOZE BULLETIN

In the nineteenth century, rum was considered excellent for cleaning hair and keeping it healthy!

FRIENDS WHO DRINK TOO MUCH

People often deny that they have drink problems because they're not ready to face up to the reality of their situation. It can make helping them very difficult indeed. Some go to great lengths to cover up the issue, and may react badly if you press them about it. Even a well-intended question can misfire badly, and you may end up encouraging them to become even more secretive about the situation.

"My boyfriend was gutted when we split up, and word began to spread that he was drinking more than usual. We were still on speaking terms but all that changed when I asked him if the rumours were true. He went ballistic, and called me a fraud for pretending to care. Months later, he phoned to say sorry. He said he had only flared up because he knew I was right."

Jessica (16)

The most effective way to approach someone who turns to alcohol for the wrong reasons is by noting the changes in their behaviour. Try to highlight the way the habit has affected their lives, rather than making them feel guilty or ashamed, and let them decide how to act on it. Here are some of the signs that suggest someone you know might have drink dependency problems. It's no guarantee, but if you recognise any of the following characteristics then it should be cause for concern.

Unusual behaviour

Only you can tell if someone you know is behaving out of character. Without further evidence, it's hard to link it to drink, but if their behaviour is unpredictable or impulsive then a dependency issue may well be behind it. They may seem distracted, or repeat themselves without realising, and timekeeping may become a problem too. This can apply to someone who is hiding the fact that they've been boozing, or simply thinking about drink and finding it hard to resist.

Mood swings

A person who relies on alcohol to feel normal may be scratchy and irritable when sober. If they have been drinking, however, then they might appear to calm down, or be more confident than usual. They may also react negatively when pressed about their alcohol intake.

Different drinking habits

A noticeable change in drinking patterns should ring alarm bells. Someone who begins to booze more than normal, or who is quick to suggest a drink may be experiencing difficulties controlling their alcohol intake. Also watch out for friends who regularly drink before going out, or turn up drunk at clubs or parties.

Mixing with a new crowd

Everyone likes making new friends. It's natural to want to expand your social circle. But if a mate has taken to boozing, and is covering up the habit, then s/he may be drawn to hanging out with people with a reputation for drinking. Alternatively, they may just 'vanish' for periods of time, and be reluctant to say where or who they've been with.

Secrecy

Nobody likes to admit that they've lost control to alcohol. It takes courage and time, and before they can face up to it they may well deny there's a problem or go to great lengths to cover it up. They might play down the issue, or promise to cut down but fail to see it through. At worst, they won't take kindly to any questioning about alcohol, and wind up making even more of an effort to keep their habit hidden from you.

"Six months ago, my best mate said he thought I was drinking too much. He had noticed me gulping my first few pints whenever we got served in the pub, and so had other friends. I was shocked, and told him to mind his own business, but deep down I knew that he was right."

Shane (16)

BOOZE BULLETIN

Every Christmas approximately 10,000 people in the UK seek help for alcohol-related problems.

DEALING WITH DRINKERS

You can't make someone quit drinking. Nor can anyone else. In every case, it's down to the person with the problem. Even so, you can still help them. Firstly, by sharing your concern, and then by offering your support as they seek to resolve the situation. Of course, it's natural to feel hesitant about raising such a delicate subject, and if you need to talk to someone about it yourself, then first contact one of the many support and advice organisations listed at the end of this book. Once you're ready, here are some of the constructive ways you can tackle the issue without risk of creating a stir:

- Choose a good moment, when you think s/he's sober and you're both calm enough to discuss things reasonably.

- Be open and honest about your concerns, but aim to highlight the problems that their drinking has caused.

- Don't make them feel guilty, ashamed or threatened, but be clear about your position. Even if they react badly, you mustn't back down.

- Give them a chance to respond, and encourage them to talk about their relationship with alcohol.

- Ask them how they would like to resolve the situation, and stress that you're willing to give them all the help and support they need.

- Suggest some strategies to help them cut down or quit drinking (see Chapter Six for more info). Also give them the number for Drinkline (0800 917 8282), but don't expect them to call straight away.

- Only a problem drinker can get their drinking under control, so give them time to consider your conversation. Try not to press them to act on their alcohol habit, as they're more likely to end up making promises they can't keep. When they're ready, they'll face up to it on their own terms. At the very least, however, talking to them about it might just be the wake-up call they need.

"It was a great help knowing that I could talk to my brother. He was the one who first pointed out that I was drinking more than normal. Had he confronted me about it, I reckon I would've denied there was a problem. As it was, he wanted to help and that gave me the courage to recognise that I had to do something about it."

Tim (16)

BOOZE BULLETIN

Approximately 30,000 deaths each year are related to alcohol in some way, making drink one of the biggest killers in the UK.

DEALING WITH EMERGENCIES

Drinking sensibly might help people to loosen up and relax, but in large amounts it can stop being fun and even become dangerous. Consuming large quantities of alcohol can lead to alcohol poisoning, respiratory and circulatory system failures, as well as choking on vomit; all of which can lead to death. Mixing alcohol with other drugs can also prove to be fatal.

If someone you know drinks too much and becomes unconscious, don't be the one who stands back helpless. Even if they simply want to lie down and sleep it off, here's what you can do to ensure they're safe and sound:

- Place them in the 'recovery position'. This means turning them on their front but with their head turned sideways to prevent them from choking should they vomit.

- Even if it looks like they are just sleeping, its important to check their breathing and make sure you can wake them up. Never leave them alone.

- If they're out for the count, and you can't rouse them, stay with them and get someone to call an ambulance.

- Check breathing while you're waiting for help to arrive, and be ready to perform mouth-to-mouth resuscitation.

- Keep them warm, but don't let them get too hot.

"I once got so drunk that I passed out. Fortunately, my mates made sure I was lying on my side. It wasn't pleasant waking up in a pool of sick, but had I been on my back I might've suffocated as a result. That was the last time I ever drank beyond my limit."

Anon

BOOZE BULLETIN

A little first aid know-how could save the life of someone who has drunk more alcohol than their body can manage. For more information, contact St John's Ambulance (0870 235 5231) or visit their website (www.sja.org.uk).

Problem pages overleaf →

WILL DRINK HEAL HEARTBREAK?

Ever since my best mate was dumped by her boyfriend, she's been really keen to go out and get drunk. I wouldn't mind too much, but she never seems to have a good time and I'm worried it's getting out of hand.

Natasha (16)

It's natural for strong emotions to follow the break up of a relationship, and your mate is clearly going through a tough time. It also sounds like she's using alcohol as a way to escape from her feelings surrounding the split. If anything, that shows she's not coping well, but as a friend you can help.

Only she can get her boozing habit under control, but sharing your concerns may at least make her think about her reliance on drink. Next time she suggests going out and getting smashed, why not suggest doing something that doesn't involve alcohol? That way you're drawing attention to her habit without being seen to criticise.

At the same time make yourself available to talk, and encourage her to open up about what's going on in her life right now. She may not give up or cut down straight away, but at the very least she'll realise that it's better to face up to her feelings about this split than to drink in a bid to blot it out.

DRUNK DATE

My boyfriend always drinks a lot at parties, but lately it's all the time. Recently we went out on a date, and I could smell beer on his breath. He denied he'd been drinking, but basically I don't believe him and I'm worried his habit's getting out of control.

Georgia (15)

People drink for all sorts of reasons, but it's down to your boyfriend to recognise that he's not just doing it to relax and unwind. All too often, telling someone they drink too much can put them on the defensive. In some cases it may even persuade them to hide their habit, which only makes things worse.

Instead, encourage your boyfriend to think for himself about why he's always boozing. Share your concern when he's sober and let him know that you're ready to talk about any deeper issues that are driving this need to drink. You may not get a response straight away, but if he's sensitive to your feelings and the future for this relationship, then at the very least it'll make him more alcohol aware.

Give him a chance to address the situation. If he continues drinking in your company, however, and you're worried about his behaviour, then consider calling time on the romance and helping him as a friend.

CHAPTER EIGHT

Living with a problem drinker

"I used to hate my dad for being a drunk. Now I just feel sorry for him."

Fiona (14)

"I always suspected my brother was a bit of a drinker, as he spent most evenings in the pub. The problems only really came to the surface when money began to go missing from Dad's wallet, and it turned out my brother had been stealing from him to buy booze."

Rick (12)

"I've lost count of the times my mum has said she'll stop drinking. I wish she would, for my sake, but I know that I can't force her."

Sue (15)

Decisions about drinking are up to you. Nobody can force you to get into alcohol, or make you cut down or quit, just as you can't expect to dictate someone else's drinking habits. But when you're living with someone who abuses alcohol, it stops being a matter of choice and becomes more like an unwanted guest. One who won't go away just by asking nicely, and can end up playing hell with your home life. Even so, that doesn't mean you're powerless to protect yourself, which is what this chapter's all about!

ALCOHOL IN THE HOUSE

Maybe you have a parent who has one or two drinks in the evening. Perhaps they've thrown a party where the booze was flowing freely. Even so, that doesn't mean there's any cause for concern. In the UK, 9 out of 10 adults use alcohol in their social activities and experience no dependency problems. Apart from the odd hangover, their drinking will have no ill effect on you or anyone else under the same roof.

"My grandma likes a drink on Christmas Day, which always means she's snoring by eight o'clock!"

Sheila (13)

BOOZE BULLETIN

It is estimated that 80,000 children in the UK are living with parents who have a serious drink problem.

FACING UP TO PROBLEMS

Living with someone who enjoys a drink is one thing. Living with a problem drinker, or an alcoholic, is a far more serious matter, and one that doesn't just affect that person. In fact, alcoholism is often called 'the family disease' because it has an impact on everyone surrounding the drinker. It's a destructive force, causing unpredictable and extreme behaviour, mood swings, lying and violence. It's also known as a 'progressive' disease. This is because the drinking problem can develop so slowly over time that you may not even notice that their behaviour is unusual. Living in this kind of environment isn't healthy. It can seriously damage your self-esteem, leave you feeling unloved, sensitive to conflict, and even shape the way you handle relationships later in life.

"Mum started drinking soon after she split up with Dad. My sister reckoned it was her way of coping at the time, but it just got worse. Eventually, we had to go and live with my dad until she sorted herself out."

Jessica (14)

If you're living under the same roof as a problem drinker, it's vital that you put your own welfare first. You can take steps to help them, but first you have to help yourself. To take stock of your situation, ask yourself the following:

- Do you feel unable to raise the issue with them, because you're scared they might react badly?
- If that person behaves unpredictably when drunk, are you or anyone else in your family at risk of harm?
- Have you skipped school to take care of them?
- Has drinking made that person a danger to themselves because of drink?

If you feel the answer is yes to any of these questions, then you need to seek outside help immediately. It may be tempting to think you can handle the situation yourself, or hope things will get better in time, but you'll be doing yourself a big favour by contacting one of the helplines or agencies listed at the back of this book. Just talking things through in confidence with a trained counsellor will help you decide what you would like to see happen to resolve things. It doesn't mean the person with the problem will get into trouble. Far from it. People will want to help, but it's down to you to ask.

BOOZE BULLETIN

In the UK, up to 14 million working days are lost each year due to drinking.

"I was worried about telling my gran what was happening at home because it felt like telling tales. When I finally found the courage to say that dad had been sacked for drinking, she gave me a big hug and said I had done the right thing by coming to her."

Paula (14)

Facing up to your feelings

It's hard to accept that someone you love has run into difficulties with alcohol. Parents, in particular, are people who aren't supposed to have problems, after all! As a result, it's only natural to feel let down by them and go through feelings of resentment, anger and even disgust. That's why it's important to stay focused on the fact that they're not boozing excessively for fun, but because they're hiding from issues in their lives they find hard to handle.

"There have been times when I've lied about my dad to friends, just to cover up the fact that he's an alcoholic. It's then that I really wish he would disappear from my life. I don't really mean it, but I get so frustrated because he won't accept that he needs help."

Damion (15)

Whatever your feelings about that person's drink habit, it's important to accept that their problem affects you, and that you deserve help too. Otherwise you risk stewing over the situation, and taking out your frustration on yourself and the people you care for.

"Mum used to try and hide the fact that she was drinking again, and that annoyed me. It was only when my girlfriend realised why I was so snappy with her that I finally opened up about the situation at home."

Errol (15)

BOOZE BULLETIN

Alcohol is a factor in up to 40% of all domestic violence incidents in the UK.

Coping with the situation

Accepting that you can't make someone close to you quit drinking is a big step. It shows you understand the situation, and can help you cope with the impact on your life. Here's how:

- If you feel comfortable sharing your concerns, and you think the problem drinker will be willing to listen, then go ahead and talk to them. Just choose a good time, when they're sober and calm. Aim to strike up a conversation about it, rather than attempting to lecture them and risking a big showdown!
- Let them know that you're uncomfortable hiding their habit from other people. That doesn't mean you plan to blab about their boozing in a bid to make them stop. It just means that next time someone asks about the situation at home you're not going to cover up or make excuses.

- Avoid trying to control their habit by hiding bottles or tipping away their drinks. It could lead to a confrontation, especially if they're drunk at the time.

"I was shaking when I told my brother that I didn't feel safe when he was drunk. I thought he would start yelling, but instead he looked utterly dumbstruck. He reckons that was what persuaded him to cut back."

John (13)

Please don't be embarrassed about turning to people outside the situation for advice and support, or feel somehow you're betraying the people you love. Everyone needs help sometimes, and even if you only feel up to talking in confidence with a telephone counsellor, this can at least help ease your anxiety. When times are tough it's always tempting to give up on them altogether and run away from home, but that won't resolve the issues you're leaving behind. Even if you feel at risk, it's vital that you seek professional assistance to help you feel safe again.

BOOZE BULLETIN

Publicans, doctors and seafarers are believed to be the most likely people to develop drink problems.

DO DRINK PROBLEMS RUN IN THE FAMILY?

There is evidence to suggest that children of alcoholics run a greater risk than others of developing drink dependency problems. Experts reckon your genetic background and the environment in which you were raised could have a big influence on your alcohol habits. Even if your parents are big drinkers, however, this does not mean that you'll become one too. A great deal comes down to your personality, peer group and mental state. What's more, research has shown that children of problem drinkers are just as likely to become committed non-drinkers as those with an alcohol-free upbringing!

> "My dad used to say he drank beer because he was thirsty. When I found out he had an alcohol problem, I felt as if he had been lying to me."
>
> **Peter (13)**

Admitting to yourself that a parent or other family member has a drink dependency problem can go a long way to ensuring that you won't follow in their footsteps. It's all too easy to deny that any problem exists, and convince yourself their relationship with drink is normal. As a result, when troubling issues arise in your own life, the instinct is to reach for the bottle just as they did. That's why it's such a big achievement to step back now from the fact that someone you love is in difficulty with drink. If you can learn to take responsibility for yourself, you'll be in a better position to help them.

"I don't drink. It's partly because I don't like the taste but mostly because I saw what it did to my mum."

Lucas (15)

BOOZE BULLETIN

Alcohol is a factor in approximately one in three UK divorce petitions. This means one partner's excessive drinking has contributed to the marriage bust-up.

REAL LIFE

Bethany's alcoholic father left home when she was fourteen. His departure sparked her own descent into drink.

My dad was an alcoholic, but nobody liked to talk about it. My family just seemed to accept that was how things were, but because it went unspoken, alcohol became a taboo subject. He split up with my mum when I was fourteen, and it was only afterwards that my family began to open up about the issue.

Alcohol taboo

My mum blamed Dad's boozing for the split, which was hard for me because at the time friends were turning up at parties with bottles of cider and packs of beer, and I liked a drink as much as anyone else.

A taste for excess

With a couple of boozy lemonades inside me, I stopped being the quiet lass who had just seen her parents go through an ugly separation. Instead, I became the girl who wasn't scared to fool around. I liked the attention. It made me forget about my home life. I don't remember the first time I got drunk on my own, but it quickly became a regular habit. My mum had taken on an evening job to support us, so she never caught me, or realised why I always had a thick head in the mornings.

School's out!

Believe me, hangovers and school don't mix! I would struggle on to first break, but after that I'd often just bunk off for the rest of the day. More often than not, I'd start drinking again around mid afternoon. It must have been obvious to everyone but me that things had got out of hand. To be honest, I didn't even think about it. For a while my friends covered for me, but eventually a couple of them went to visit my mum. One evening, I came home in my usual state and found her waiting for me. I could see she had been crying. I knew why she had taken time off work, too. I just sensed that she had sussed me, and didn't know what to say.

Coming clean

I didn't just come clean to my mum that evening. In telling her that I had a drinking problem, I was admitting it to myself too. Discovering that I'd run into the same difficulties as Dad nearly destroyed her. It horrified me, too! That's why I agreed to go for counselling. During these sessions, I learned to cope with my feelings

*surrounding the split instead of trying to blot them out.
It took a while, and I wouldn't like to say drink is history,
but I do feel better equipped to deal with the temptation.*

Breaking free

*If anything, the experience helped me understand what
a powerful grip alcohol can have. People forget that it's
a drug. One that can easily take over your life if you start
to rely on the buzz to feel normal. Even my dad has
decided to seek help for his drink problems. My mum
reckons I set him an example. I only hope he follows
my lead!*

CHAPTER NINE

Contacts

"I didn't feel judged and nobody talked down to me. The advisor spoke my language, and left me much happier about dealing with the situation at home."

Matilda (14)

Here's hoping this book has gone some way to helping you wise up about drink, drinkers and drinking. The more you understand about alcohol, from the physical effects to the impact on the people around you, the easier it is to make informed decisions about its role in your life.

Knowing the facts also means knowing where to turn for help, now or at a later date. Whether it's more info you're after for yourself or for others, confidential counselling or just a friendly chat, you'll find the cream of the crop listed here.

Al-Anon and Alateen
Provide understanding, strength and hope for anyone whose life is, or has been, affected by someone else's drinking. Contact the helpline, or write to the address below, for details of groups in your area.
61 Great Dover Street
London SE1 4YF
Helpline: 020 7403 0888

Alcoholics Anonymous
Fellowship of men and women who aim to help each other recover from alcoholism. Local branches can be found in the phone book, or contact:
PO Box 1, Stonebow House
Stonebow
York YO1 7NJ
Tel: 0845 7697 555
www.alcoholics-anonymous.org.uk

Alcohol Concern
Huge resource bank of information on all aspects of alcohol use and abuse, including details of local counselling services.
Waterbridge House
32-36 Loman Street
London SE1 OEE
Tel: 020 7928 7377
www.alcoholconcern.co.uk

British Association of Counselling
Tel: 01788 578328
A register of professionally trained counsellors in your area. Call for details, or search the database at www.counselling.co.uk

Careline
Tel: 020 8514 1177
For anyone who would like to talk to a trained counsellor about any issue that's troubling them.

ChildLine
Freephone: 0800 1111
Trained counsellors provide advice for children on any issue that concerns them. Calls are free and won't appear on the phone bill. You can also write to ChildLine
Freepost 1111
London N1 0BR
(no stamp needed)

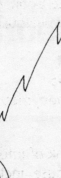

Drinkline
Tel: 0800 917 8282
National helpline offering confidential support and advice if you're worried about your own or someone else's drinking.

Samaritans
Tel: 08457 90 90 90
www.samaritans.org.uk
Confidential emotional support for any person who is suicidal or despairing.

Think about drink
www.wrecked.co.uk
Facts about alcohol for young people, including the chance to suss out your weekly unit intake.

Victim Support
Tel: 0845 30 30 900
Support and information for victims of crime, such as alcohol-related violence.

Visit www.learn.co.uk for more resources

learn.co.uk
from *The*Guardian

Index

Another Wise Guide

BULLYING

Michele Elliott

Nearly everyone is bullied at some point in their life. But what exactly does bullying mean? Are there practical things you can do to stop it? How do you deal with your anger and frustration? How can you learn to make friends and respect yourself? If you're a bully, can you ever change your behaviour?

Don't suffer in silence. Learn how to beat the bullies and restore your self-esteem with this essential wise guide.

DIVORCE AND SEPARATION

Matthew Whyman

Are your mum and dad splitting up?
What does a divorce actually involve?
How can you cope with your feelings?
What happens if a parent meets
someone new?
What is it like living with a stepfamily?

This essential wise guide gives you
down-to-earth and reassuring advice to
help you through your parents' divorce.

Another Wise Guide

DRUGS

Anita Naik

What are drugs?
What do they do to your mind –
and your body?
Are you under pressure to take drugs?
Do you have friends who already do?
What are the risks – and how should
you deal with them?

Alcohol and amphetamines, tobacco and
cannabis, solvents and steroids – know
the realities and explode the myths with
this essential wise guide.

EATING

Anita Naik

Do you worry about your weight?
Do you wish you looked like a supermodel?
Are you always on a diet?
Does eating make you feel guilty?

From crash diets and calorie-counting to
anorexia and bulimia – find out the facts
about food and you, and learn to love your
body with this essential wise guide.